# POETRY FOR KIDS

## SOPHIA SHAH

Illustrated by
Nandkumar Parab

A book by a child for a child!!



Written By: Sophia Shah
Illustrated By: Nandkumar Parab



Audience: Grade Pre-K to 8
ISBN: 978-1-7361385-2-6
Library of Congress Control Number: 2023905621
Text copyright © 2023 by Sophia Shah
Image copyright © by Nandkumar Parab
Publisher: Hiren Shah

# Foreword

We are all different — and that's a reason to celebrate! That's why Sophia Shah wrote this book of poetry for you. She wants all of us to feel welcome and at home wherever we are.

In this collection, you will find a range of poems that embrace Sophia's curiosity on various topics and explore what it means to be inclusive, to celebrate differences, and to stand up for what is right. Sophia has written these poems from her own unique perspective, drawing on her own experiences and insights to create a heartfelt and authentic work.

As we all know, diversity, equity, and inclusion are vital values that help to make our world a better place. They remind us that we are all different, and that those differences are something to be celebrated, not feared. Through poetry, Sophia has captured the essence of these values and brought them to life in a way that is both accessible and inspiring.

 I hope that this collection of poems will serve as a source of encouragement for readers of all ages. May it inspire us all to embrace diversity, seek equity, and practice inclusion in all aspects of our lives.

Lily Medina
Director of Diversity, Equity, and Inclusion Seattle Country Day School

POEMS:

Introduction

# Introduction

As a child, I always find wonders in the world around me. Like the essence of time or the senses of the human body, and the fact that I live next to a lake. Well, I really wanted to put my thoughts into words and share those words with people around the world. So, I authored poems about all these wonderful curious things in the hope of bringing in the same curiosity, joy, and happiness to my readers. I hope you enjoy my poems, thank you!


~Sophia

# As the time drifts

As the hours pass
Days to years
Either you are,
Watching the rain drops, rolling down the window.
Or you are bouncing and flipping
Be you alone or not
Observe the time pass...
Watch the sand
Quietly, timelessly
Run through the hourglass
As the sand drips
The time passes
Mystifying
Those who ponder it
As years whiz by
Or seconds seem to be months
Quiet but quick
Unnervingly astounding
Is the how and the what of time
As the sand runs
Quietly, timelessly
Through the hourglass tonight
As all else is silence.

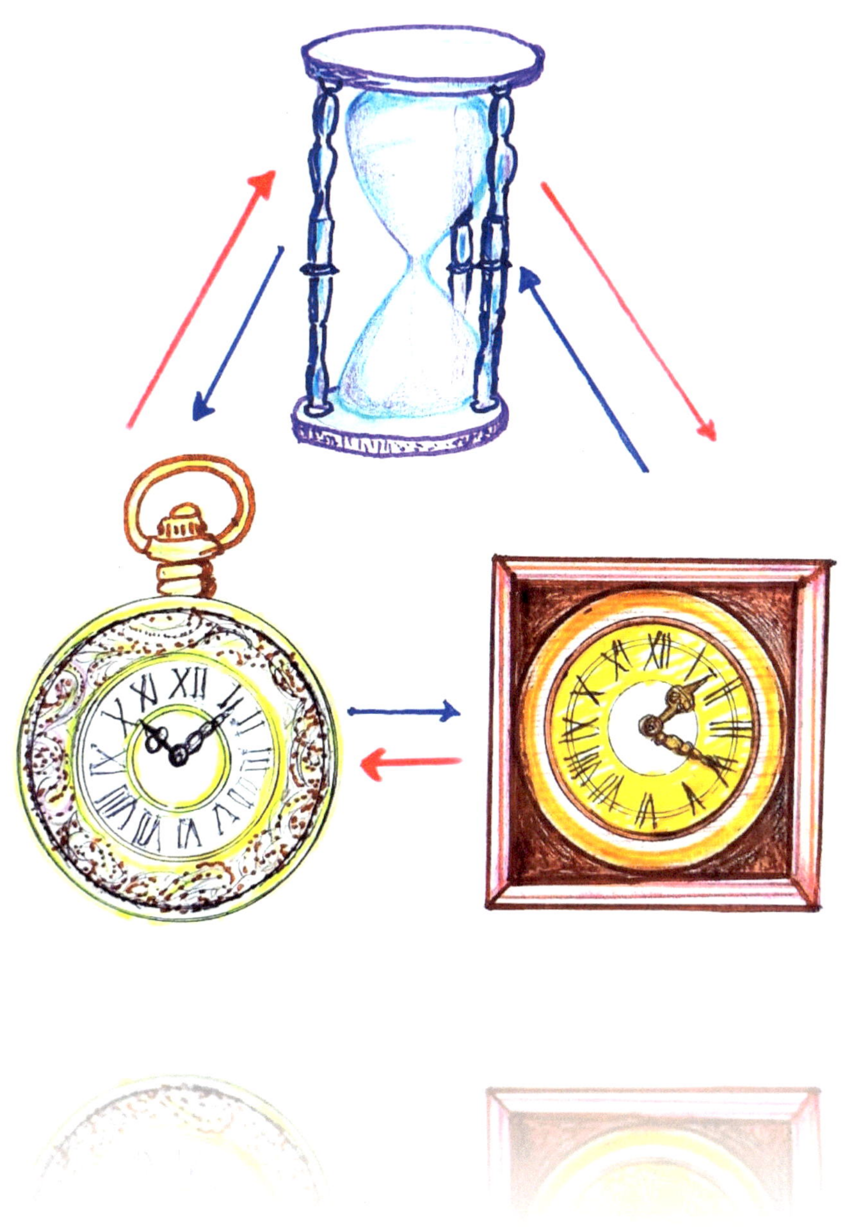

# The old Lady...

The old lady sits in deep hunter pits
and in the pits, she knits
and down there with her in the deep, shadows,
water and sunlight seep and creep to her
while she sits and knits in the deep!

Then dirt chucks up to bits,
but she still sits and knits
even with the dirt bits
then from the ground the dirt bit seems to stay and sit,
but the lady keeps sitting and knitting

She knits model shoes and even model number twos
She tries to choose which is better, shoes or twos?
she wants to choose the model number twos not the shoes
But she has shoes and two blues in her knitting

And there you can see the old lady
sitting and knitting, sitting, and knitting, sitting, and knitting...
she seems to love and enjoy... her sitting and knitting!

# Queen

Once on Halloween I saw a Queen
And what a Queen she had been
From sailing in the seas
To eating peas...
She had brown shoes
And heard the cow moos!
She said her name was Sally
She had grown up in a valley
And it took her no time to rally
She had a pet snake named Grake
And he ate cake!
She was charged loans
And heard tons of groans!

# Home: 11/09/2021

I see my breath in the air
The boats blow their horns.
My Big Blue mansion
Seagulls Squawking music to my ears.
This is where I belong....
Home, a home, my home

The big, tall house across the street
Lovely nature, flowers galore and autumn leaves
Seaview.
Puffy white clouds drifting across the sky,
The sweet smell of lavender.
Harmony to my eyes
To me to me to me
This is where I belong...
Home, a home, my home

The home
Home, Home
Home is Home

# Today at The Marina

The water sparkles
Like a Crystal
A diamond Mountain Snow-capped
Huge and peaceful.
The Sun glinting
Shining happiness
Big puffy, white clouds in the sky
Seagull's,
Questioning and answering cries.
Sea air, salt smell, ocean waves
A gentle breeze blowing across my face
The life I live next to the water.
There is a free open world...Ah life!
Today, oh today.... at the Marina.

# Autumn

See my breadth in the air
Feel the leaves crack-crack-cracking
Under my bare feet
Apples so ripe
Pumpkins so common
Halloween is coming near...
The cool breezy breeze
Blow, blow, blowing across my face,
Red from the cold!
The squirrels collecting nuts
Birds singing hoarsely
The sky
White...
Cloudy, very, very, cloudy
Autumn
Leaves all gold-red-orange-brown
Disappearing green
Autumn...
Fall...
Home...

# Spring

In the air
Smell the lavender!
A cool breeze washes over me
Like a cloud
The flowers and sound
The happy cheers!
Feel it in your bones,
It is springtime!!

Life grows, life blooms
Flowers and fruits spring up
Nature leaves behind its gloom
Birds chirp sooner
Sounding music
Sun begins to make a zoom
Its springtime

The lavender
The breeze!
Amen, new trees!
It is a beautiful time
To be alive
Don't we all agree?
Feel love and pureness

# You are a girl

You are a girl
Proud, strong, and brave
You defend the good
Rosa Parks was just a woman …….
but she ended bus segregation
You will do something amazing
something else standing in power
You, as one will change the world
who knows!
You could defend us
You could unite us
and that is because
You are a girl!
Misty Copeland was told she could never dance again
but she did
She is famous
She is a rebel girl
She changed the world
You will too
Maybe you will invent something beautiful
maybe you'll join the Navy
but no matter what you do
You are a girl
and that is enough to make you a hero
So, remember
You are not alone
She is also a girl
You could work together and change the world
and that is because
You are a girl

# You are your kind

Who are you and where do you come from?
If you are a person of color,
That doesn't make you better or worse
It just makes you, you
Your skin does not justify you, nor does it do the opposite
Your culture and your heritage define part of you but does not limit you
There is no perimeter how you should live
You matter

YOU

ARE

UNIQUE

# UNITY

Hand in hand
Heart to heart
I see you
Not with my eyes
But with my heart.
We feel a bond
We see eye to eye
We stick up for each other
We truly understand
We are united
We are strong
We are FRIENDS
After all,
Where would the world be without friendship?

UNITY

# Diversity Equity Inclusion for kids

No D.
Everyone is the same.
An incomplete world
D
No E
Nothing fair?
An incomplete world
D.E
No, I
Someone left out.
An incomplete world
We need DEI!!

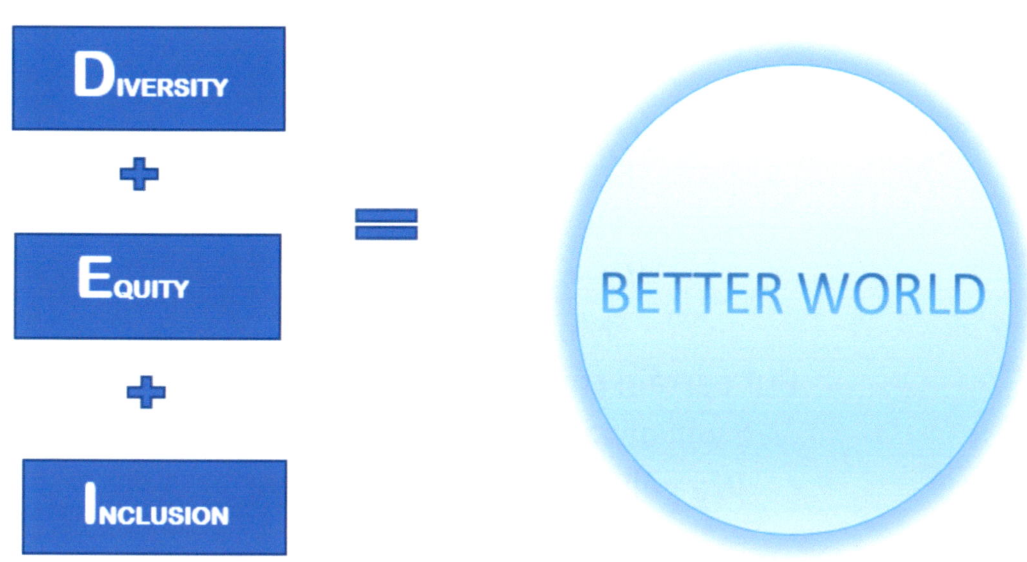
DIVERSITY
+
EQUITY
+
INCLUSION
=
BETTER WORLD

# Together We Shall Rise...

Aiden is small
But he will grow
He will change
Wiser and Stronger
More learned
But certain things are not to change
We will always have a special bond
We will always see eye to eye
We will grow together
He will grow and change
But I will always love him!!

# Textures

I can feel a tiny grain of sand
Fall between my lonely fingers
Rough...
May it be
Nor the smooth blades of grass
Could be falling rain drops
Or a hand of a lost friend
You may feel emotions
Their textures are actions
Anger is tough
Sad's mellow
Take a moment please my friend
To observe everything around you,
Its moralism and your serenity,
Feel
Live
strive...
And notice what is around you
But don't forget to feel, feel the texture,
Feel the texture... it is the wonderous thing......texture

2nd part:
May I feel textures of the world
May I discover the feel of new things
No matter how where I go, or how I strive,
I shall always feel the simple pleasures of various textures

What shall await behind that old door?
I may live, I shall learn, maybe recreate but!
It is not ever replenishable, but runs and flows
It is the texture of my life.
May it last long,
And may I feel and see the...
Texture

# Taste, Touch, Hearing, Sight and Smell

A mysterious thing it is...

Taste: a fountain of anger in lemon juice, happy chocolate, sorrow, a mellow chili, or bell pepper

Touch: Grandmas hand, an anaconda, dirt, a world of feel to haste for blossom

Hearing: A creek, bangs, bells, the water drowned our wells, Sand slithers through our lives...

Sight: A world, tragedy, fantasy in disbelief, we see wonders

Smell: Smoke, wood, food, earth, battling as it is

Be shall it say all five senses enchant out lives and bless our homes
Truly nothing shall every copy or destroy.
Taste, Touch, Hearing, Sight or Smell...
Truly nothing shall every copy or destroy.
Taste, Touch, Hearing, Sight or Smell...

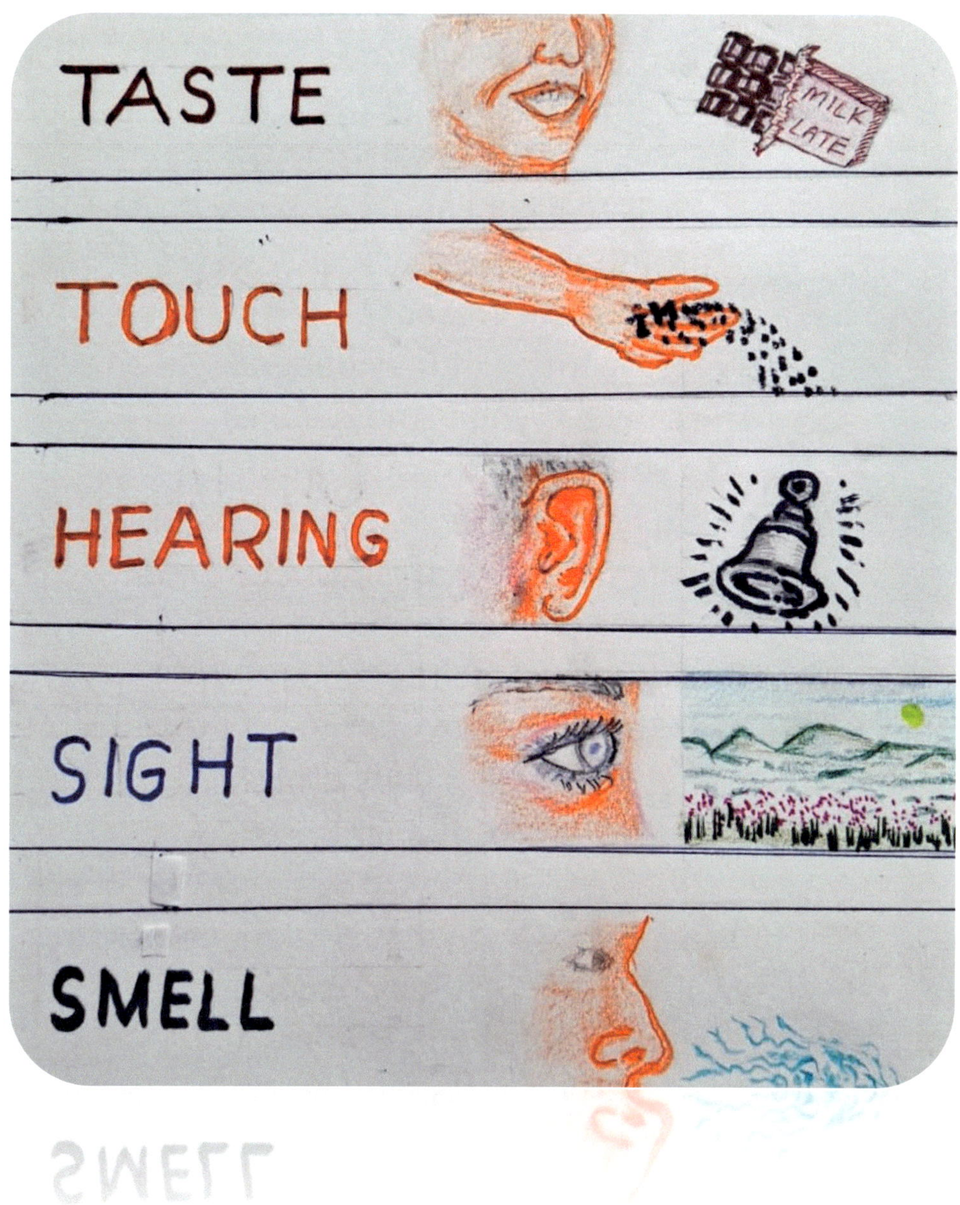
TASTE
MILK
LATE
TOUCH
HEARING
SIGHT
SMELL

# What is real?

What is real and what is fake?
Is fake to clone?
Is real facts?
Is fake lies?
Is real knowledge?
Is fake imaginary?
Is real present?
Well, my friend, it may depend
The choice is yours and belongs
To you to you to you to you
To no one else, just you!
Every person on this planet
Has a unique definition
Of things which neither you nor I
Should or may clarify
What you think is your choice
No wrong, no right
For...
What is real and what is fake?
Well, my friend, it may depend,
Though the choice is yours
You may believe your way and
Neither you nor I may judge
The answer to the
Perceiving, puzzling questions:
What is real and what is fake?

REAL

FAKE

# It is an arch of true magic

It is an arch of true magic
It is the colors worthy as day!
The sight gives hope
The shine is bright
The pureness is overdue
To symbolize true beauty,
Which is inside of you.
It disappears and glides
Leaving worlds of joy and peace
We relish and protect
The beauty of rainbow
As for the sight...
It is an arch of true magic

# As if we couldn't overcome

As if there was a moment
Of complete depression
That we couldn't break
As if we controlled lightning
A moment
We felt we couldn't make do
The big question is "how to get through"

It may seem a miserable world
But we will get up, we will fight

Just look at all the happy memories
We made together
We cannot forget them,
Listen
To me,
Get your favorite things
Depression is away
Look at what you love!
We will get back up now

As if
There was a moment we were not strong
We can do anything; move on
You can't cling to sorrow forever, come on, we can do anything.
Overcome all sorrows
Believe. Believe
As if we couldn't overcome
As if we couldn't overcome

# If there was a new world

If there was a new world out there
What would it be?
Course, it wouldn't have no variety
Shall it be an open plain, a castle or a hut!?
Should it lest be protected,
The doors kept shut?

What a world, to explore
The lore of adventure or severe calm,
The lull of rain or a
Hurricane!

There could be anything in this newfound fantasy,
We all know what is down below? Canyons, mountains,
Oceans, tall or deep? Our hidden fantasy.

If there was a new world out there,
What would it be?
Course, variety but else!
What shall it be like, where it will be
Our hidden fantasy!
We all have one.
It is called creativity, imagination, and glee!
Everyone's unique definition of the questions,
"If there was a new world out there. What would it be?"
"If there was a new world out there. What would it be?"

new
world

# About the Author

Sophia is an enthusiastic 9-year-old who loves to imagine and create. She has been authoring stories and poems since she was 6years old. She loves creating extensive stories, characters, and detailed plots. She also loves to write poetry and believes that poems are a window to one's soul. She is looking forward to authoring more books helping her imagination find a home while sharing her creativity and thoughts with kids around the world.

# About the Illustrator

Nandkumar Parab is Sophia's Grandfather who has been a skilled artist from a noticeably young age. His father and mother both were artists themselves who inspired and supported him to draw and paint. He was extremely excited to illustrate this book for his granddaughter and found the experience rewarding and special.

Made in the USA
Monee, IL
07 July 2026

56553285R00029